RIDGEVIEW UNIT SCHOOL DISTRICT NO. 19
COLFAX, ILLINOIS   61728

Music, Music for Everyone

by Vera B. Williams

MULBERRY BOOKS • New York

With thanks to Savannah
for her help

First Mulberry Edition, 1988   10 9 8 7 6 5 4 3 2 1

Library of Congress Cataloging in Publication Data

Williams, Vera B.   Music, music for everyone.
Summary: Rosa plays her accordion with her friends
in the Oak Street Band and earns money to help her
mother with expenses while her grandmother is sick.
[1. Family life—Fiction.   2. Bands (Music)—Fiction.
3. Grandmothers—Fiction] I. Title. PZ7.W6685Mu 1984   [E]
83-14196   ISBN 0-688-07811-7

Our big chair often sits in our living room empty now.

When I first got my accordion, Grandma and Mama used to sit in that chair together to listen to me practice. And every day after school while Mama was at her job at the diner, Grandma would be sitting in the chair by the window. Even if it was snowing big flakes down on her hair, she would lean way out to call, "Hurry up, Pussycat. I've got something nice for you."

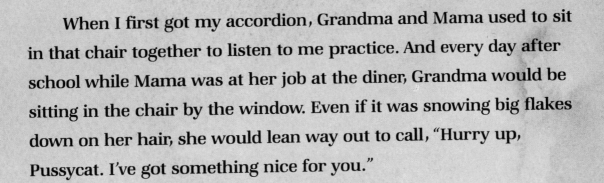

But now Grandma is sick. She has to stay upstairs in the big bed in Aunt Ida and Uncle Sandy's extra room. Mama and Aunt Ida and Uncle Sandy and I take turns taking care of her. When I come home from school, I run right upstairs to ask Grandma if she wants anything. I carry up the soup Mama has left for her. I water her plants and report if the Christmas cactus has any flowers yet. Then I sit on her bed and tell her about everything.

Grandma likes it when my friends Leora, Jenny, and Mae come home with me because we play music for her. Leora plays the drums. Mae plays the flute. Jenny plays fiddle and I play my accordion. One time we played a dance for Grandma that we learned in the music club at school.

Grandma clapped until it made her too tired. She told us it was like the music in the village where she lived when she was a girl. It made her want to dance right down the street. We had to keep her from trying to hop out of bed to go to the kitchen to fix us a treat.

Leora and Jenny and Mae and I left Grandma to rest and went down to get our own treat. We squeezed together into our big chair to eat it.

"It feels sad down here without your grandma," Leora said. "Even your big money jar up there looks sad and empty."

"Remember how it was full to the top and I couldn't even lift it when we bought the chair for my mother?" I said.

"And remember how it was more than half full when you got your accordion?" Jenny said.

"I bet it's empty now because your mother has to spend all her money to take care of your grandma till she gets better. That's how it was when my father had his accident and couldn't go to work for a long time," Mae said.

Mae had a dime in her pocket and she dropped it into the jar. "That will make it look a little fuller anyway," she said as she went home.

But after Jenny and Leora and Mae went home, our jar looked even emptier to me. I wondered how we would ever be able to fill it up again while Grandma was sick. I wondered when Grandma would be able to come downstairs again. Even our beautiful chair with roses all over it seemed empty with just me in the corner of it. The whole house seemed so empty and so quiet.

I got out my accordion and I started to play. The notes sounded beautiful in the empty room. One song that is an old tune sounded so pretty I played it over and over. I remembered what my mother had told me about my other grandma and how she used to play the accordion. Even when she was a girl not much bigger than I, she would get up and play at a party or a wedding so the company could dance and sing. Then people would stamp their feet and yell, "More, more!" When they went home, they would leave money on the table for her.

That's how I got my idea for how I could help fill up the jar again. I ran right upstairs. "Grandma," I whispered. "Grandma?"

"Is that you, Pussycat?" she answered in a sleepy voice. "I was just having such a nice dream about you. Then I woke up and heard you playing that beautiful old song. Come. Sit here and brush my hair."

I brushed Grandma's hair and told her my whole idea. She thought it was a great idea. "But tell the truth, Grandma," I begged her. "Do you think kids could really do that?"

"I think you and Jenny and Leora and Mae could do it. No question. No question at all," she answered. "Only don't wait a minute to talk to them about it. Go call and ask them now."

And that was how the Oak Street Band got started.

Our music teachers helped us pick out pieces we could all play together. Aunt Ida, who plays guitar, helped us practice. We practiced on our back porch. One day our neighbor leaned out his window in his pajamas and yelled, "Listen, kids, you sound great but give me a break. I work at night. I've got to get some sleep in the daytime." After that we practiced inside. Grandma said it was helping her get better faster than anything.

At last my accordion teacher said we sounded very good. Uncle Sandy said so too. Aunt Ida and Grandma said we were terrific. Mama said she thought anyone would be glad to have us play for them.

It was Leora's mother who gave us our first job. She asked us to come and play at a party for Leora's great-grandmother and great-grandfather. It was going to be a special anniversary for them. It was fifty years ago on that day they first opened their market on our corner. Now Leora's mother takes care of the market. She always plays the radio loud while she works. But for the party she said there just had to be live music.

All of Leora's aunts and uncles and cousins came to the party. Lots of people from our block came too. Mama and Aunt Ida and Uncle Sandy walked down from our house very slowly with Grandma. It was Grandma's first big day out.

There was a long table in the backyard made from little tables all pushed together. It was covered with so many big dishes of food you could hardly see the tablecloth. But I was too excited to eat anything.

Leora and Jenny and Mae and I waited over by the rosebush. Each of us had her instrument all ready. But everyone else went on eating and talking and eating some more. We didn't see how they would ever get around to listening to us. And we didn't see how we could be brave enough to begin.

At last Leora's mother pulled us right up in front of everybody. She banged on a pitcher with a spoon to get attention.

Then she introduced each one of us. "And *now* we're going to have music," she said. "Music and dancing for everyone."

It was quiet as school assembly. Every single person there was looking right at Leora and Jenny and Mae and me. But we just stood there and stared right back. Then I heard my grandma whisper, "Play, Pussycat. Play anything. Just like you used to play for me."

I put my fingers
on the keys and buttons of
my accordion. Jenny tucked
her fiddle under her chin.
Mae put her flute to her
mouth. Leora held up her
drums. After that we played
and played. We made mistakes,
but we played like a real band.
The little lanterns came on.
Everyone danced.

Mama and Aunt Ida and Uncle Sandy smiled at us every time they danced by. Grandma kept time nodding her head and tapping with the cane she uses now. Leora and Jenny and Mae and I forgot about being scared. We loved the sound of the Oak Street Band.

And afterward everybody clapped and shouted. Leora's great-grandfather and great-grandmother thanked us. They said we had made their party something they would always remember. Leora's father piled up plates of food for us. My mama arranged for Leora, Jenny, and Mae to stay over at our house. And when we finally all went out the gate together, late at night, Leora's mother tucked an envelope with our money into Leora's pocket.

As soon as we got home, we piled into my bed to divide the money. We made four equal shares. Leora said she was going to save up for a bigger drum. Mae wasn't sure what she would do with her share. Jenny fell asleep before she could tell us. But I couldn't even lie down until I climbed up and put mine right into our big jar on the shelf near our chair.